OTHER YOUNG YEARLING BOOKS BY

ICS
ang
es,
ol-
st.
d-
ad
of

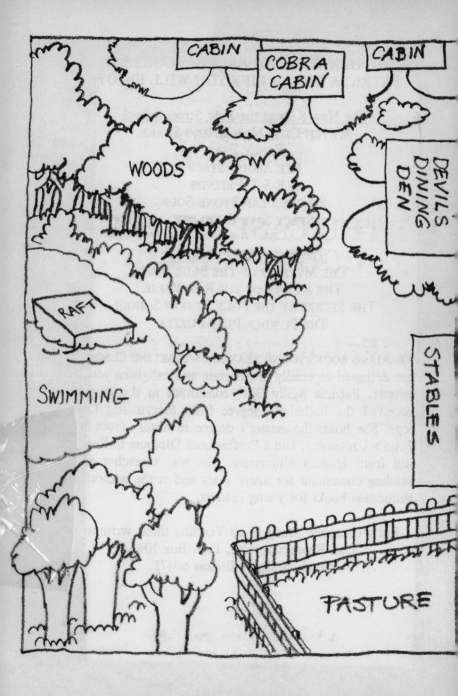

THE POLKA DOT
PRIVATE EYE

# THE CASE OF THE COOL-ITCH KID

## Patricia Reilly Giff

## Illustrated by Blanche Sims

A YOUNG YEARLING BOOK

Published by
Dell Publishing
a division of
Bantam Doubleday Dell Publishing Group, Inc.
666 Fifth Avenue
New York, New York 10103

ISBN: 0-440-40199-2

Printed in the United States of America

July 1989

10 9 8 7 6 5 4 3

W

*To Rosalinde, Logan, Joey, Ryan and
Carrie Lynn Flammer, with love*

# THE CASE OF THE
# COOL-ITCH KID

# ···CHAPTER 1···

Dawn Bosco looked around her room. "What a mess."

Boxes were all over the place.

So were clothes.

Orange and white T-shirts.

A shiny red bathing suit.

Blue plaid socks.

"Hurry," said Noni, her grandmother. "Get dressed. Everything has to go into the suitcase."

Dawn sat on her bed. "I think I changed my mind."

1

Her mother popped her head in the door. "Camp day. Camp Wild-in-the Woods."

"I guess I'm not going after all," said Dawn.

"Just think," said Noni. "Swimming in Lake Wild-in-the-Woods.

Dawn shivered. "Snakes."

"Walks in the woods," said her mother.

"Bears," said Dawn.

Noni looked up at the ceiling. "Horse-back riding."

"I forgot about that," Dawn said.

"Cookouts with marshmallows," said her mother.

"You're right," said Dawn.

She pulled on her Polk Street School T-shirt.

She yanked on her sneakers.

She stood up and hopped over her suitcase.

She landed on her Polka Dot Detective Box.

2

The box sailed across the room.

Dawn sailed with it.

She banged her head on the floor.

"Ouuuu-ch."

"Rub it hard." Noni clicked her teeth. "Why are you taking that detective box anyway?"

"I never went to western camp before."

Noni smiled. "You never went to any camp."

"I know." Dawn swallowed. "That's why I have to take everything."

Dawn's father came down the hall. "Hurry. You'll miss the bus."

"Ready?" asked Noni.

Dawn looked around. "Not ready."

Noni sighed. "Now what?"

"My hat. The one that says POLKA DOT PRIVATE EYE."

"The bus is across the street," her brother,

4

Chris, yelled. "It's in front of the Polk Street School."

"Hurry," yelled Noni.

Dawn crawled under her bed.

Not there.

She dived into her closet.

Last winter's boots were there. An old coloring book. Her tulip costume.

She held up the costume. "Maybe I'll bring—"

"There isn't even room for a toothpick," Noni said.

Dawn reached deeper into her closet. "Here!"

She shoved the hat into her detective box.

She took a breath. "Now I'm ready."

Her father picked up her suitcase.

"I think the bus is leaving," said her mother. "Run."

Noni reached out. "Quick. Take this. It's a Remember Me Bag."

"Thanks." Dawn grabbed the paper bag. She raced down the hall.

"Don't open it until there's nothing to do," Noni called after her.

Dawn sped down the stairs.

"Don't miss that bus," Chris said. "My summer will be ruined."

Dawn wrinkled her nose at him.

She whooshed up her mouth.

It was her anteater face.

Then she dashed out the door.

She could see the bus. It was red. The license plate was the same as her house: 195.

Jill Simon stuck her head out the bus window. "Hurry," she screamed.

Dawn raced across the street. She climbed up the steps of the bus.

Her father handed her the suitcase.

"Wait," she said. "I think I forgot something."

Too late.

The doors closed. The bus started up.

## ···CHAPTER 2···

Dawn headed down the aisle.

She pushed her suitcase ahead of her.

She passed Miss Perry, the counselor.

Miss Perry was as skinny as a pretzel. She winked at Dawn and waved her whistle.

The bus was filled with girls.

Not one boy.

That was because Camp Wild-in-the-Woods was a girls' camp.

Almost all the girls were wearing blue T-shirts.

They said COOLIDGE SCHOOL.

Dawn sounded it out.

Cool-Itch.

The Cool-Itch Kids didn't look friendly.

No, not friendly at all.

Dawn bumped down the aisle.

"I saved you a seat," Jill Simon yelled.

"Coming." Dawn sighed. Jill Simon was the only girl she knew.

Dawn wished some other girls from her class had come, too.

Everyone else had something to do.

Emily was at her grandmother's house.

Sherri was at the beach.

Linda had a sprained wrist.

Dawn gave her suitcase a push.

It smashed into a girl's leg.

"Watch out, Polk Street." The girl had a fresh face with a pointy nose.

Dawn gritted her teeth. "I'm trying, Cool-Itch."

She slid into the seat next to Jill.

Jill smiled at her. "I'm the one who always bumps into things."

Dawn smiled back. Jill was a good friend.

She had four braids, a round face, and a huge western hat.

Dawn clicked her teeth.

She wished she had thought of a western hat.

What else had she forgotten?

Something.

She couldn't think of it, though.

Dawn wished she had a window seat.

She leaned across Jill.

It was hard to see.

The window was cracked . . . cracked like a spider web.

Someone yelled, "Time to sing."

Dawn turned around.

It was a girl with a thousand freckles.

"I always go to this camp," said the girl. "I know all about it." She opened her mouth. " '*Home. Home on the range . . .*' "

Dawn sang, too.

She was glad she had a nice loud voice.

She banged the top of the seat in front of her.

*Where the deer*—BANG
*And the an-te-lope play.*
BANG. BANG.

The fresh face kid turned around. "In a minute I'm going to punch you in the nose."

Fresh Face looked big. She looked strong.

Dawn stopped banging.

She sat back and closed her eyes.

She was sick of this ride.

It was bumpy.

It was taking forever.

It was time to look at Noni's Remember Me Bag.

11

There was nothing else to do.

She pulled out the fat paper bag. It was tied with green wool. "Good stuff in here," she told Jill.

Jill leaned over. "Something to eat, I hope."

Dawn untied the wool. She dug into the bag.

A package of butterscotch candy with a note: "Brush your teeth after this."

Homemade chocolate chip cookies.

A pink and purple I LOVE MY GRAND-MOTHER pin.

And best of all, a mirror . . . a mirror with beautiful beach shells around the edge.

"Gorgeous," said Dawn.

"Lucky," said Jill.

"Double lucky," someone said. It was a girl with gold fingernails. She was leaning across the aisle.

Dawn reached deeper into the bag. "There's more, I think."

"Rest stop," called Miss Perry.

Bump! The bus stopped to let them out.

Dawn handed a butterscotch candy to Jill.

She shoved one in her own mouth.

She put the bag on her seat. They'd look at the rest later.

Outside, everyone began to run around.

Some kids played hide-and-seek.

Some kids went into the girls' room.

The rest lined up at the Triple Dipple Gum Machine.

"That's for me," said Jill.

Dawn shook her head. "I need a drink."

She stood in line in back of Fresh Face.

She made an anteater face when Fresh Face wasn't looking.

Then Miss Perry blew her whistle.

It was time to get back on the bus.

The bus drove around the circle to meet them.

It bumped over the curb.

It screeched to a stop.

Dawn climbed up. She stopped at her seat. "You first," she told Jill.

"Look," Jill said.

Dawn looked down.

Her Remember Me Bag was a mess.

Things were all over the floor.

"Oh, no," she said.

"Oh, no," Jill said, too.

They scrambled to pick things up.

A pink swirly pencil.

A box of Cool Cat writing paper.

The pink and purple I LOVE MY GRAND-MOTHER pin was gone.

So was her mirror . . . her beautiful beach shell mirror.

A chocolate chip cookie had a bite in it.

14

Dawn swallowed. She felt like crying.

Jill looked as if she were going to cry, too.

"Horrible," Dawn said. She held up the cookie with two fingers. "How could anyone eat my food?"

"Maybe someone was hungry?" Jill said.

"Gross," said Dawn.

"Very hungry?" Jill asked.

"No," said Dawn. "They should have asked." She frowned. "There's a thief on this bus. A grandmother pin thief. A beach shell mirror thief."

Jill's lip was quivering. "A real thief?"

"Of course, a real thief," said Dawn.

She looked around. It was a good thing she was the Polka Dot Detective.

She had a mystery to solve.

And as soon as she solved it, she was going straight home!

16

# ···CHAPTER 3···

The bus driver beeped his horn.

"Here we are," yelled Miss Perry.

Dawn looked up.

She saw old wooden gates, a bunch of cabins.

Where were the horses?

Where was the lake?

Everyone piled off the bus.

Everyone but Dawn.

She wanted to check out the rest of the bus.

Maybe she'd find a clue.

She'd catch the thief. One two three.

Miss Perry stuck her head back inside.

Her whistle blasted.

Dawn jumped a foot.

Miss Perry grinned at her. "All out," she said.

Dawn took one more quick look. Then she rushed off the bus.

Ahead of her, Miss Perry moved fast. "Smell that great Wild-in-the-Woods air," she said.

Dawn took a deep breath.

Wild-in-the-Woods air smelled like regular old air to her.

Miss Perry pointed. "Our horses. They love to race for miles."

Dawn looked. Three horses were standing in the middle of a field.

They were fat and falling asleep.

They probably couldn't even walk a block.

In back of her the know-it-all girl with a thousand freckles was whispering.

"Hurry," Dawn heard her tell Fresh Face. "We want to get the best bunks."

Dawn marched fast.

Know-It-All and Fresh Face moved faster.

Dawn sped up.

She tried to pull Jill along.

Jill was huffing and puffing. She kept banging into everything.

They rushed up the hill . . . and through the woods.

Straight ahead was a log house.

The sign said: COBRA CABIN.

"Horrible," said Dawn.

She started up the steps.

She crossed her fingers.

She hoped there'd be a huge color TV inside.

She wanted fat pink pillows on the beds.

Then she raised her shoulders in the air.

Who cared about pillows?

Who cared about a TV?

She was going to get back her pin and her mirror, and find out who ate her cookie.

Then she was going to go home.

H-o-m-e, home.

Miss Perry threw open the doors. "Pick your bunks."

No rugs were on the floor, no curtains.

There were plain old pillows and a skinny mini black-and-white TV.

A bunch of bunks lined the walls. Bottom bunks and top ones.

A long, skinny aisle went down the middle. Yucks.

Know-It-All and Fresh Face were racing for the first bunks.

Dawn raced, too.

She was dying for a top bunk.

Know-It-All and Fresh Face got there first.

Dawn dived for the next one.

"Too bad," said the girl with gold finger-nails.

Dawn looked around.

All the bunks were taken.

"Over here," yelled Jill.

She was jumping up and down in front of the end bunks. They were all the way back by the wall.

Jill's western hat covered her eyes.

Dawn raced over. "I'll take the top."

Jill pushed her hat up. "I never had a top bunk in my life."

Dawn put her hand on the ladder.

"Besides," said Jill, "I got here first."

Dawn took her hand off the ladder.

She wanted to make an anteater face.

She couldn't do that.

Jill was her only friend in this whole place.

She sank down on the bunk.

It was hard as the sidewalk.

The pillow felt like the Polk Street School hamburgers.

Jill started up the ladder.

CLUNK!

Her western hat sailed past.

Dawn jumped. "What was that?"

"Me," said Jill. "I tripped a little."

"Too bad you didn't give me the top." Dawn said it in a little voice.

She didn't want to hurt Jill's feelings.

She started to look around for the thief.

A girl was hanging off a top bunk across the aisle. "Ex-er-cise," she yelled.

The girl with the gold fingernails was painting her toes gold.

Someone else was pasting double heart stickers on the wall.

Dawn looked over at Fresh Face.

She looked like a thief.

Besides, she had crumbs all over her mouth.

Dawn leaned over.

She'd get out her Polka Dot Detective Box.

She'd work on the crime right now.

"Oh, no," she said.

The box wasn't there.

She had left it home.

She sank back on the bunk.

Now it was going to be twice as hard to find the Cool-Itch thief.

# ···CHAPTER 4···

Dawn could hardly open her eyes the next morning.

She yawned seven times on the way to breakfast.

Jill had cried all night.

She kept saying she wanted to go home.

Miss Perry was up all night too. She kept patting Jill's shoulder.

"Some baby always cries," said the know-it-all girl.

Dawn was glad no one thought she was a baby.

She was glad no one knew she had cried, too.

She couldn't stop thinking of her mother and father and Noni.

"Don't think about it now," she told herself. It was time for breakfast. Time to solve a crime.

She marched into the Devil's Den Dining Room.

Jill marched with her.

So did the rest of the girls from Cobra Cabin.

Other campers were there, too.

The noise was terrible.

People were yelling.

Plates were banging.

"Here's our table," said Miss Perry.

Dawn slid onto the bench next to Jill.

She looked at the plate in front of her. It was a horrible yellow plastic thing. It had a white line across the center.

"What's that?" she asked.

"Glue," said Know-It-All. "Get-it-together glue. Everything around here is falling apart."

Dawn sighed. She couldn't wait to go home.

"Where do they get all the glue?" Jill asked. "I need some."

Know-It-All raised one shoulder. "It's all over the place. It's in the closets. In the drawers. Everywhere."

Miss Perry began to fill the glasses.

"I bet it's strawberry," Dawn said.

Know-It-All shook her head. "It's old GJ."

Dawn looked at her plate.

She wasn't going to ask what GJ was.

She was getting sick of Know-It-All.

She picked up her glass. It shouldn't be hard to guess anyway.

She tasted it. Not bad.

She took another sip.

"What's GJ?" Jill asked.

"Garbage juice, of course," said Know-It-All. She leaned forward. "They strain it right out of the garbage pail."

"Of course." Dawn put her glass down again.

"Don't be silly," said Miss Perry. "It's mixed fruit juice."

A woman came with a platter.

The middle was filled with lumpy scrambled eggs.

Around the edge was something else.

It looked like turkey.

Who would eat turkey for breakfast? Dawn thought.

She looked closer.

No, it wasn't turkey.

It wasn't anything she had ever seen.

"What is it?" Jill asked.

"Old TG," said Know-It-All.

Dawn closed her eyes.

She didn't even want to find out.

"What's—" Jill asked.

"Tuna guts," said Know-It-All.

"I thought so," said Dawn.

"It is not," said Miss Perry.

"Well, what is it?" asked Know-It-All.

"I don't know exactly," said Miss Perry. She started to laugh. "Meat, I hope. Good healthy meat."

Dawn looked around.

There was nothing else but bread and butter. The bread was tan. The butter had crumbs all over it.

Just then the woman came with a bowl of apples.

Everyone dived for one.

Dawn and Fresh Face grabbed for the last one.

"Mine," yelled Dawn.

"Mine," yelled Fresh Face. She opened her mouth for a huge bite.

Dawn drew in her breath.

There was something on Fresh Face's T-shirt.

It was a pin.

A pink and purple I LOVE MY GRAND-MOTHER pin.

# ···CHAPTER 5···

Lake Wild-in-the Woods was cold. Freezing.

The bottom was muddy.

No one else seemed to mind, though.

Fresh Face and the Ex-er-cise Girl were swimming around like crazy.

Jill was doing a doggy paddle.

Her head was high above the water.

She didn't want to get her western hat wet.

Dawn went as fast as everybody else.

Her arms curved over her head.

They dipped down into the water.

Her feet stayed flat on the bottom, though.

She couldn't swim one bit.

She could hardly float.

For a while she circled around Fresh Face.

It was a good thing she was a detective, Dawn thought.

Fresh Face hadn't guessed she had seen the pin.

Dawn could just keep watching.

Sooner or later she'd find out where her gorgeous shell mirror was.

Then she'd grab the pin.

She'd grab the mirror.

She'd tell Miss Perry that Fresh Face should be arrested.

Then she'd call Noni one two three.

She'd be home in no time.

Perfect.

After a while she got tired of waving her arms around.

She waded out of the water.

She checked to make sure there were no snakes hanging around in the grass.

Then she sat down.

She wished she could speed things up a little.

She was sick of waiting around for something to happen.

Then she sat up straight. She had thought of something.

Just then Jill came out of the water. She pulled off her western hat and squeezed out her braids.

"Listen," said Dawn. "Sit down. I want to tell you—"

"Sit down? Are you crazy? With a million snakes probably . . ." She stopped for a breath. "And those things with the legs . . . hundreds of legs."

"Will you listen? There's something we have to do."

Jill nodded. "You're right. We have to eat. I'm starving to death."

"No, not that. Something else. We're going to sneak up to the cabin."

"Sneak? Why don't we just walk?"

"We're going to search. We'll look in the closet. We'll—"

"Nothing in the closet. Just a bunch of glue and blankets."

Dawn raised her shoulders. "We'll look in the beds. Under the— " Dawn broke off.

Jill looked as if she were going to cry.

"What's the matter?"

Jill shook her head. "Nothing."

"You're afraid," Dawn said. "Afraid of a silly thief."

Jill stuck out her lip.

"Good grief." Dawn closed her eyes.

"Why are your eyes closed?" Jill asked.

"I'm waiting for you to listen."

Jill's lip quivered. "I am listening."

Dawn raised one hand. "Don't be afraid for a minute. Just follow me."

She looked around.

No one was watching.

She was looking up at the sky.

She picked a little blue flower.

She kept backing up toward the trees.

She stopped to take a quick look at Jill.

Jill was taking huge tiptoe steps.

One hand was out for balance.

The other covered her mouth.

Dawn gritted her teeth.

Everyone in the water must be watching.

She stood there.

What should she do?

Then she darted back into the trees.

Let everyone watch that silly Jill.

In the meantime, she'd take a good look at the cabin.

She raced up the path.

Her feet were bare.

The pebbles hurt.

She tried not to pay attention.

She climbed the three wooden steps.

Inside she went straight to Fresh Face's bunk.

She looked under the pillow.

Nothing there but an old fur cat.

Half the tail was missing.

Fresh Face had probably stolen it from some poor baby.

Dawn ran her hands over the blanket.

Smooth.

Nothing hidden under there.

Maybe underneath.

Yes, something.

A box with cats all over it.

It reminded her of something.

What?

Just then the door burst open.

Something peered in the door.

A horrible something.

It had no hair on its head.

Its eyes were huge and strange.

Dawn backed away from it.

Something was in the way, though.

A suitcase.

She threw out her arms.

She couldn't stop herself.

She was sliding, falling.

And the thing was coming closer.

# ···CHAPTER 6···

"Who's screaming like that?" Dawn asked. "Who's making all that noise?"

"You," someone said.

"Oh." Dawn looked up.

A circle of faces was looking down at her.

Jill.

The Ex-er-cise Girl.

Gold Fingernails.

Jill helped her up. "What happened?"

"Something horrible." Dawn's knees were shaking.

"I hope you're not going to cry," said Know-It-All. "Some big baby is always—"

Dawn drew herself up. "Not me. I don't cry. I never—"

"I think I heard you last night," said the Ex-er-cise Girl. "I heard somebody."

"Get to the something horrible," said Gold Fingernails.

"It had no hair. It had big eyes. Green, I think. Or maybe gray."

"No such thing as a ghost in this camp," said Know-It-All.

"I want to go home," Jill said.

"Good thing Miss Perry was out on the raft," said Gold Fingernails. "You're not supposed to be in here."

Fresh Face stared at Dawn.

She squeezed her eyes together into little slits. "Yes," she said. "What are you doing here?"

Dawn looked around.

Everyone was staring at her.

Everyone was waiting.

She opened her mouth.

She tried to think of something to say.

"Wait a minute," said Know-It-All. "What was that noise?"

"I heard it, too," said Gold Fingernails.

"It's Miss Perry's whistle," said Jill. "Hurry. We have to get dressed."

A few minutes later, everyone dashed out of the cabin.

Everyone but Dawn and Jill.

"I want to go home," Jill said again.

"Me, too," said Dawn. "I'm writing to Noni. Right this minute."

"Tell her to get me, too," said Jill.

Dawn nodded. "Don't worry."

Miss Perry's whistle was getting closer.

Dawn reached under her bed quickly.

She pulled out the pink swirly pencil.

She grabbed a piece of Cool Cat writing paper.

Now they could hear Miss Perry's voice. "Time for a snack," she was saying. "Isn't everyone starving?"

Jill looked at Dawn. "I wonder what it is."

"Probably GJ," said Dawn. She pulled her shirt over her head.

"Maybe it's something good," Jill said. "Marshmallows."

Dawn shoved the swirly pencil over her ear.

She stuck the Cool Cat writing paper in her pocket.

They raced outside.

Everyone was standing around Miss Perry.

She was handing something out of a box.

Dawn stood on tiptoes to see.

"It's old CC," said Know-It-All.

"Chocolate cook . . ." Jill began.

Know-It-All shook her head. "Caterpillar crunch."

Dawn backed away from everyone.

She went around to the back of the cabin.

She took a good look at the grass and the rocks.

No snakes.

No horrible things.

She sank down on a log and pulled out the Cool Cat paper.

DEAR NONI:

COME AND GET ME.

GET JILL TOO.

THIS PLACE HAS TERABUL FOOD.

IT HAS HARIBLE THINGS.

IT HAS A THIEF.

LOVE AND KISSES,

DAWN BOSCO

44

P.S. I NEVER GOT TO RIDE THE
HORSE.
P.S. AGAIN. I DON'T EVEN HAVE MY
POLKA DOT DETECTIVE BOX.

"I knew it," said a voice behind her.
Dawn looked up.
It was Fresh Face.
She was wearing a black hat.
It had fur all over it. A long tail hung
down the neck.
"I am the Cool Cat Detective," said Fresh
Face. "And you have stolen my Cool Cat
detective paper."

# ···CHAPTER 7···

Dawn stood up.

She put her hands on her hips.

She put her nose up close to the Cool-Itch Detective.

"You have some nerve," she said. "One, you are wearing my pink and purple I LOVE MY GRANDMOTHER pin. Two, I'm a detective, not a thief. I'm the Polka Dot Private Eye."

Fresh Face blinked.

Dawn opened her mouth again.

Then they both started to talk at once.

". . . my pin," said the Cool-Itch Detective.

". . . my initials on the back," said Dawn.

". . . my writing paper," said Cool-Itch. "My special Cool Cat black-and-white writing—"

"My gorgeous mirror with the beach shells all over—" Dawn broke off. "My chocolate chip cookie. You took a big bite."

Cool-Itch shuddered. "I hate chocolate."

They stopped for a breath.

"Will you please get your nose out of my face?" said the Cool-Itch Detective.

Dawn sat down on the log again.

The Cool-Itch Detective sat down, too. "What's your name anyway?" she asked.

"Dawn Bosco. Just look at the back of the pin. You'll see it. D. B."

The Cool-Itch Detective pulled at the pin. "You'll see in one second," she said. "No name. No letters."

"What's your name?" asked Dawn.

"Lizzie Lee." She pulled off the pin. "Hey."

Dawn leaned over and looked at the pin. She straightened up. "You are now the Cool-Itch Thief."

Lizzie Lee scratched her head. "D. B. You're right."

"Of course, I'm right," said Dawn. "What do you think . . . I made this whole thing up?"

"Hmm," said Lizzie Lee. "I guess I made a mistake."

Dawn was about to say, "You certainly did."

She didn't, though.

She had thought of something else.

She leaned forward. "We've got a horrible thing at this camp. It sneaks into the cabin—"

"No hair?" asked Lizzie. "Green eyes?"

"You saw it, too?"

Lizzie took a deep breath. "I'm the horrible thing. I have a bald wig. I have a mask with green eyes. It's stuff from my detective box."

Dawn opened her mouth. Then she closed it again. If only she had her own detective box.

"I didn't take your pin," said Lizzie Lee.

Dawn looked at her.

Lizzie Lee didn't look so fresh anymore.

"I didn't take your paper either," said Dawn.

"We could team up," said Lizzie. "Find out about your pin . . . and my writing paper."

"And my beach shell mirror?"

Lizzie nodded.

Dawn thought for a minute.

Why not?

I guess so," she said. "But I'll be the main detective."

Lizzie put her hands on her hips. "Unh-unh," she said. "Both the same."

"Well . . ."

"Besides, I have a great idea."

Dawn didn't have an idea.

Not one.

"All right. Both the same."

She leaned over.

She couldn't wait to hear the idea.

# ···CHAPTER 8···

It was dark.

Black.

Dawn opened her eyes wide.

She still couldn't see.

She had a Cool-Cat Detective Flashlight. She couldn't turn it on, though.

Not yet.

She and Lizzie Lee were sneaking out of the cabin.

Outside, it was noisy.

They could hear crickets and tree frogs.

Dawn walked on tiptoes.

She didn't want to step on anything. Snakes, or lizards, or crackly things.

In a minute they were in the woods.

In front of her Lizzie stopped. "Which way? We don't want to get lost."

Dawn shivered.

She wished she had remembered a sweater.

If only she had her Polka Dot Detective Box.

It had a compass inside.

She just had to learn how to use it.

She looked around. "I see a light. That way."

"You sure?" Lizzie asked.

Dawn crossed her fingers. "Of course."

They marched toward the light. "See," Dawn whispered. "There's the flagpole. There's the gate. . . ."

"Whew," said Lizzie. "And there are the buses."

They started to run toward them.

The parking lot looked strange at night. Tall lights with mist around them.

Pale buses.

"Which one?" Lizzie asked.

Dawn pointed. "I remember the number. One-nine-five."

"Good detective work," said Lizzie.

"You're right," said Dawn. She had never thought of that.

They pushed open the doors.

"Can you remember where you sat?" Lizzie asked.

"Of course." Dawn looked for the window with the cracks like a spider web.

"Now," said Lizzie. "My idea."

"Our idea," said Dawn.

"Yes. The Cool-Cat Detective Book says start at the beginning."

"That's what the Polka Dot Detective

Book says." Dawn crossed her fingers again. She couldn't remember what her detective book said.

"Think about the beginning," said Lizzie.

Dawn squinched her eyes shut tight. "I had everything here on my seat. All my stuff."

Dawn opened her eyes.

Lizzie's eyes were shut. "My Cool Cat writing paper was on my seat."

"I was sick of the ride," said Dawn.

"Me, too," said Lizzie. "All the bumps."

"Then we stopped," said Dawn. "Everyone got off the bus."

"Drinks of water," said Lizzie.

"Triple Dipple Bubble Gum," said Dawn. She frowned. "I know what happened."

"What?" Lizzie asked.

"The bus went over a bump before it picked us up."

"Everything fell off the seat," said Lizzie.

"When we picked up the stuff . . ."

"You're right," said Lizzie. "It got all mixed up."

She held out her hand. "Shake. Great detective work."

Dawn shook her head. "Not such hot work. Not even a great mystery."

"Not a mystery at all," said Lizzie.

Dawn knelt.

She ran her hand under the seat. "My shell mirror must be right here."

She could feel something under her fingers.

She reached for it.

Just a piece of shell.

No mirror.

She sat back on her heels, thinking.

Who had taken that mirror?

Who had taken a bite of the cookie?

Just then there was a sound.

The bus door.

It began to open quietly.

Dawn could feel her heart pound.

"Who's there?" yelled Lizzie Lee.

The door banged shut.

Someone began to scream.

Dawn scrambled to her feet.

In the mist it was hard to see.

"Look," she said.

A shape. Someone moving across the parking lot.

Someone she knew?

Yes.

But who?

# ···CHAPTER 9···

Miss Perry blew her whistle. "It's a great day, everyone. Open your eyes."

Dawn opened one eye.

It couldn't be morning yet.

She had just gotten to sleep.

She'd been dreaming . . . dreaming about running.

Something kept catching her feet.

Glue.

A whole parking lot filled with glue.

Dawn opened the other eye.

Yellow patches shone on the cabin wall.

Miss Perry was right. It was a beautiful day.

Dawn sat up straight.

She snapped her fingers. "I've almost got it. I've almost solved the crime."

"Oh, no," said Lizzie Lee. "I wanted to solve it first."

In the bunk above, Jill turned over. "Too tired," she said.

"Wake up, lazybones," Miss Perry said.

Lizzie Lee jumped out of her bunk. "Tell me," she said to Dawn.

Dawn pulled a comb through her hair. "I don't exactly have it. Not yet, I mean. I know it has to do with glue."

"Today is Wednesday," said Know-It-All. "The best breakfast. It's pancakes."

Dawn was starving.

She rushed out of the cabin with the others.

They headed for the Devil's Den Dining Room.

"Tell me about the mystery," said Lizzie. "I'll help you finish it up."

Dawn raised her shoulders in the air. "It's about the glue. I just can't—"

"Remember what the Cool-Cat Detective Book says."

They said it together: "Go back to the beginning."

Dawn stopped walking.

She closed her eyes. "In the bus—"

"I'm sick of the beginning," said Lizzie. "Try to remember the middle part."

"What's the middle?" Dawn climbed the steps into the dining room.

Inside, the pancakes smelled wonderful. Almost as good as Noni's. Dawn thought for a minute. "Last night," she said. "That's the middle. We went into the bus. We found a broken shell."

She slid into her seat.

She poured a gallon of syrup on her pancakes. She shut her eyes. "Someone went back into the bus. Someone took my mirror."

"Someone broke your mirror," said Lizzie.

Dawn nodded. "Someone who likes cookies."

She opened her eyes. "Oh, no. I've just solved the mystery."

Jill looked up. She had a ring of syrup around her mouth. "Oh, no," she said, too.

"Oh, yes," said Dawn. "Jill Simon. My only friend."

"Not your only friend," said Lizzie Lee.

Jill put a huge piece of pancake in her mouth.

At the same time she started to cry.

Dawn felt like crying, too. "You went back into the bus."

"It was scary, very scary." Jill took a breath. "I had to do it, though."

"But what . . . how?" Lizzie Lee began.

'I went back that first day, too," Jill said. "Back for my wallet. I wanted to buy a piece of Triple Dipple Bubble Gum."

"You took a bite of my chocolate chip cookie," Dawn said.

Jill took a gulp of milk. "I just love—" She broke off. "I was going to tell you. I knew you wouldn't mind."

Dawn nodded.

"But then . . ."

Lizzie Lee leaned closer.

Jill put down her glass. She swiped at her mouth. "I sat on your mirror."

"Oh, no," said Dawn.

"Only a little bit," said Jill. "I was going to fix it one two three."

"But then . . ." Dawn said.

65

"I had to get the glue." Jill sighed. "Then I had to find the missing shell."

Dawn nodded.

"But something horrible was inside the bus," Jill said. "I couldn't get—"

Dawn and Lizzie laughed. "We were the horrible thing," said Lizzie.

And Dawn said, "Don't worry. I've got the shell. We'll fix the mirror together."

Know-It-All leaned over. "I'll help. I'm good at that kind of stuff. I learned it here at camp."

"I'm sorry," Jill said. "Really sorry." She mopped up the last of her pancake. "I guess we can go home now."

"Go home?" Lizzie asked.

"Go home?" Dawn said.

She took another bite of her pancake.

They were as good as Noni's.

Definitely.

The door opened.

Someone came in with a package.

"Special mail for Dawn Bosco," the woman said.

"Wow," said Lizzie. "It's as big as a whale."

"I hope it's food," said Jill.

Dawn shook her head. "I think I know."

She started to tear open the paper.

She could see pink polka dots. She could see a note.


DEAR DAWN:

HERE IS YOUR POLKA DOT DETECTIVE BOX.

I PUT SOME CHOCOLATE CHIP COOKIES INSIDE.

LOVE,

NONI

P.S. HOW'S THE HORSEBACK RIDING?

Dawn looked at Jill. "Horseback riding. I nearly forgot."

"Horseback riding starts on Thursday," said Know-It-All. "It always does."

"We'd better not go home," said Jill.

"No." Dawn wiped her mouth. "Besides, I have my detective box now. We might find another mystery to solve."